ROCK AWAY GRANNY

by Dandi Daley Mackall
illustrated by Mike DeSantis

Sky Pony Press
New York

Sky Pony Press books may be purchased in bulk at special discounts for sales promotion, corporate gifts, fund-raising, or educational purposes. Special editions can also be created to specifications. For details, contact the Special Sales Department, Sky Pony Press, 307 West 36th Street, 11th Floor, New York, NY 10018 or info@skyhorsepublishing.com.

Sky Pony® is a registered trademark of Skyhorse Publishing, Inc.®, a Delaware corporation.

Visit our website at www.skyponypress.com.

10 9 8 7 6 5 4 3 2 1

Manufactured in China, December 2016

This product conforms to CPSIA 2008

Library of Congress Cataloging-in-Publication Data is available on file.

Print ISBN: 978-1-5107-0835-8
Ebook ISBN: 978-1-5107-0836-5

Cover design and illustrations by Mike DeSantis

For my dancing granddaughters,
Ellie, Cassie, and Maddie—Rock on!
—DDM

To dancing Grandma Terry
and Papa Phil
—MD

We drive to Granny's—she's always there,

Just rock, rock, rockin' in her rocking chair.

My mom says,
"Honey, I've got to go.
You rock with Gran.
Keep the rockers slow."

Boring
    rock,
        rock,
            rock
at Granny's house tonight.

There's no TV, and I miss my toys.

Our squeaky chairs make the only noise.

I watch Mom leave, and I feel the blues.

Then Gran tap-taps in her blue suede shoes.

Gonna rock, rock, rock at Granny's house tonight.

The rockers stop, and she paints my nails.
She combs our hair into pony tails.

"It's time to rock!" But I don't know how.

She grabs my hand. Then she takes a bow,

Whispers, "Rock, rock, rock at Granny's house tonight!"

We get out records—they're small and black.

A guy named Elvis has a giant stack.

She lifts my arms like they're on a spring.

We make the "bridge" to the West Coast Swing.

Swing and rock, rock, rock at Granny's house tonight.

"Squirm side to side like you've just been kissed.

Well, look at you! You can do the twist!"

Now . . .

Side Pass,

Anchor Step,

Underarm Turn,

Cuddle,

Tunnel,

Octopus,

—anyone can learn.
I can rock, rock, rock
at Granny's house tonight!

The boogaloo has a boogie beat.

Gran takes the lead. I just watch her feet.

I slide and guide. Then I swirl and twirl.

My gran grooves out like a go-go girl!

And we rock, rock, rock at Granny's house tonight.

We do the swim with a *splish, splish, splash.*

Our feet *stomp! stomp!* It's the Monster Mash.

My mom's still gone. I don't mind the wait.

At Granny's house, we can stay up late!

'Cause we rock, rock, rock at Granny's house all night.

I'm fading fast, so I think I'll stop.

"Just one more, dear? It's the Bunny Hop.

Now, kick one leg. Kick the other, too.

Then hop, hop, hop, like the bunnies do."

Hop and rock, rock, rock at Granny's house tonight.

I'm all danced out, so we both retire
To rocking chairs by the burned-out fire.

When Mom comes back and my granny's snoring,

Mom whispers, "Hon, was it just too boring?"

But we rocked, rocked, rocked at Granny's house tonight.

We kiss goodnight. How I hate to go!

Then I *shuffle, shuffle, shuffle* off to Buffalo.

GRAB SOME FRIENDS AND DO
THE BUNNY HOP!

Form a line behind the leader. Hold on to the waist of the person ahead of you while you groove around the dance floor in one long train.

Just follow these simple steps:

1. Kick your right foot twice.
   (Hey—don't kick the kid in front of you!)
2. Kick your left foot twice.
3. Hop forward one jump.
4. Hop backward one jump.
5. Hop forward three times.

1.

2.

3.

HOW TO ROCK AND ROLL!

The best thing about dancing rock and roll:

It's so much fun that you have to do it with a smile on your face.

Usually, you'll be dancing with others who have smiles on their faces, too.

Great music!

You can't do it wrong (even if you mess up the steps)!

4.   5.